To my champions,
Roger Di Paolo
Tom Stephan
Rose Mary Piazza Stehman-Humble

— D.D.

For Henry

— A.R.

GO!

ISBN 978-1-338-27152-2

12 11 10 9 8 7 6 5 4 3 2   18 19 20 21 22 23

Printed in the U.S.A.   08

This edition first printing, January 2018

Typography by Adam Rex and Dana Fritts

Long ago,

in an ancient and distant realm called
the Kingdom of Backyard,

there lived a warrior named

ROCK.

Rock was the strongest in
all the land, but he was
sad because no one could
give him a worthy challenge.

Rock traveled to
the mysterious Forest
of Over by the Tire Swing,
where he met a warrior
who hung on a rope,
holding a giant's underwear.

Even though he had won, Rock was still unsatisfied.

So he journeyed on, to the mystical Tower of Grandma's Favorite Apricot Tree.

There he was met by an odd and delicious fruit.

ARE YOU NOT ENTERTAINED?!

They *were* entertained.

But the battle had been too easy. So Rock left the Kingdom of Backyard, still in search of a worthy foe.

Meanwhile,
in the Empire of Mom's Home Office, on lonely and windswept Desk Mountain, a second great warrior sought the glory of battle.

And his name was Paper.

Even though he was the smartest warrior in all the land, he was also sad, because no one could outwit him.

He set out across Desk Mountain to find his match. There he met a large and square monster.

Having beaten the fiercest fighter of Desk Mountain, Paper climbed down to the Pit of Office Trash Bin, where he battled the most terrifying horde of creatures in all the land . . .

PAPER

VERSUS

HALF-EATEN

BAG OF

TRAIL

MIX!

And so, with a heavy heart, Paper departed the Empire of Mom's Home Office.

At the same time,

in the Kitchen Realm,

in the tiny village of Junk Drawer,
there lived a third great warrior.

They called her Scissors,

and she was the fastest blade in
all the land. She, too, was unchallenged.
On this day, her first opponent was a
strange and sticky circle-man.

Scissors forged on across the Kitchen Realm
to the frigid wastes of Refrigerator/Freezer.
There she met her most fearsome adversaries yet . . .
dinosaurs made of frozen breaded chicken.

AM I SO GOOD THAT NOT EVEN DINOSAUR-SHAPED CHICKEN NUGGETS CAN BE BEAT ME?

And so Scissors, like Rock and Paper before her, traveled beyond her own kingdom, seeking out a challenger who was her equal.

Then one day,
in the great cavern
of Two-Car Garage,

Rock and Scissors
came face-to-face.

An epic
and legendary battle
ensued, but ultimately …

ROCK
IS VICTORIOUS!

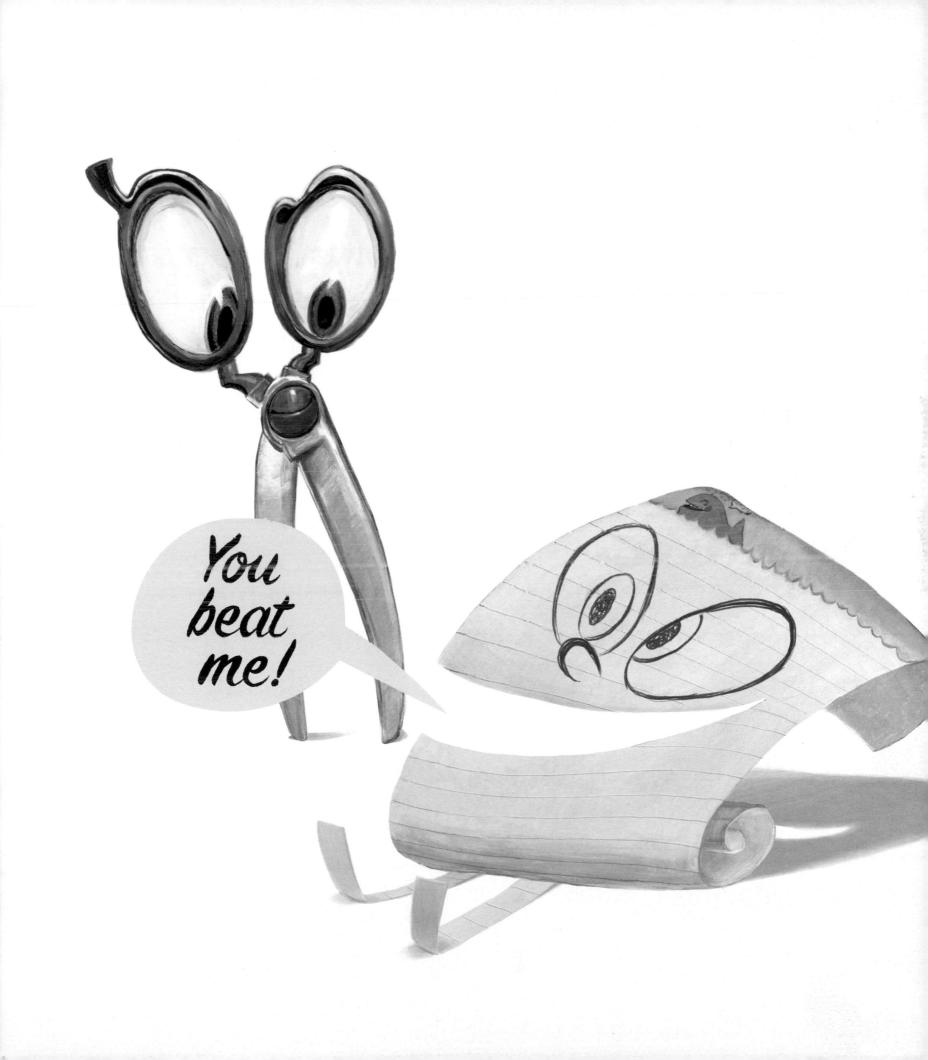

And the three great warriors hugged each other and danced for joy, and they became fast friends.
Finally, they had each met their matches. They were so happy, in fact, that they began to battle again.

'Round and 'round they went, in the most massive and epic three-way battle of all time! And it is said that this joyous struggle still rages on to this very day.

That is why children around the world—in backyards, on playgrounds, and yes, even in classrooms—still honor the three great warriors by playing . . .

ROCK, PAPER, SCISSORS!